The House of Bricks

Retold by Annette Smith
Illustrations by Colby Heppell

Three little pigs lived in a house with their mother.

You are big now. You can't live here.

2

So the three little pigs
went off into the forest.

The three little pigs
made their houses.

The next day,
a big bad wolf
came out of the forest.

He saw the straw house.

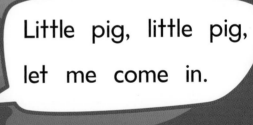

Little pig, little pig,
let me come in.

So the wolf huffed,
and he puffed, and he blew
the straw house down.

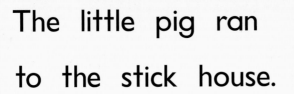

The little pig ran
to the stick house.

A big bad wolf is coming.
Please let me in.

The little pigs ran inside
and shut the door.

9

The wolf looked in the window of the stick house.

Little pigs, little pigs, let me come in.

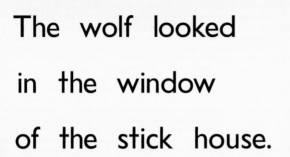

So the wolf blew
the stick house down.

The two little pigs
ran to the brick house.

The wolf is coming.
Please let us in.

The wolf raced
up the path
to the brick house.

Little pigs, little pigs,
let me come in.

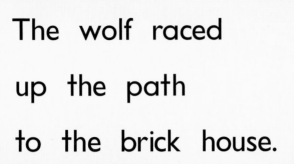

The wolf huffed, and he puffed, but the brick house did not fall down.

15

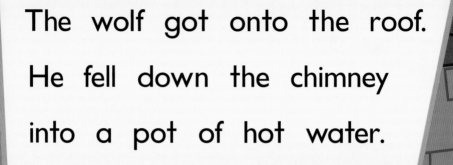

The wolf got onto the roof. He fell down the chimney into a pot of hot water.

That's the end of the big bad wolf.